Disney's
THE NEW ADVENTURES OF
WINNIE the POOH
Eeyore's Tail Tale

TWIN BOOKS

MALLARD PRESS

Eeyore sighed, watching Rabbit hop around his garden. Rabbit was chasing bugs, but Eeyore thought he was dancing.

"Wish I could dance," said Eeyore.

Eeyore tried to copy Rabbit's dance step, but he stepped on his tail and fell.

"Not again!" Eeyore said, annoyed. That tail of his was forever coming off, and he was pretty tired of it.

He rose and walked away, leaving his tail in the mud.

Rabbit charged into his carrot patch. "All right, you pests," he said, grabbing his bug sprayer. "You asked for it!"

He sprayed until there was a billowing cloud covering his garden. When it cleared, the garden seemed to be deserted.

"Where'd those little bugbarians go?" asked Rabbit. Suddenly, the bugs appeared behind him with a big board.

Thwack! The bugs knocked Rabbit over the fence. He landed in the mud next to Eeyore's tail.

"Ick!" said Rabbit, wiping the mud off his face. When he sat up, he saw an army of bugs marching towards him, aiming the bug spray in his direction.

"Oh, dearie dear!"

Rabbit frantically searched for something he could use to defend himself. When he spotted Eeyore's tail, he snatched it up.

"Don't come any closer!" warned Rabbit, swinging the tail. "I've got...er...THIS!"

To Rabbit's surprise, the bugs came to a complete halt. The leader's eyes nearly popped out, and his heart beat wildly. He howled and whistled, and started trembling all over. Then, before Rabbit could blink, the leader of the bugs ran up to Eeyore's tail and hugged it to his tiny body. Obviously, it was love at first sight. But what could a bug see in Eeyore's tail?

"Hmm!" said Rabbit thoughtfully. "This gives me an idea." And he took the tail off to his house.

By now, Eeyore was beginning to miss his tail. For one thing, he was a lot colder back there.

Suddenly, Tigger bounced up and knocked Eeyore flat.

"Hoo-hoo-HOO! Hiya, Donkey Boy! Say, I almost didn't recollect you without your tail."

"We parted company at Rabbit's," explained Eeyore. "I'm much happier without it. Can't you tell?"

Tigger studied Eeyore's face, which looked as gloomy as ever.

"How'll you be able to tell your front from your back without a tail?" asked Tigger. "And since you're always sayin' you're such a nobody, won't you be even less of a somebody with part of you missin'?"

The corners of Eeyore's mouth drooped a little lower.

"You're right. But, how can I get the little guy back?"

"Hoo-hoo! Have no fear—Private Ear Tigger is here! And reunitin' loved ones is what Private Ears do best!"

Back at Rabbit's house, Eeyore's tail had taken on a new look. Using bits of paper and some glue, Rabbit turned Eeyore's tail into a lady caterpillar.

"Now that's what I call a Worm Wrangler!" said Rabbit, sticking Eeyore's tail on the end of a fishing pole. Then Rabbit dangled the tail in front of the bugs and led them to a stream.

"Good-bye! Have a wonderful trip!" called Rabbit, waving to them as they sailed downstream in a shoebox.

Later, Winnie the Pooh knocked on Rabbit's door.
"Hello, Pooh," said Rabbit. "How are you this great day?"
Pooh saw the tail dangling from Rabbit's fishing rod.
"What's that?" asked Pooh.
"This? Oh, nothing," said Rabbit, as he quickly hid the fishing rod behind his back. Rabbit didn't realize that Eeyore's tail had dropped off. "Now, excuse me, Pooh," said Rabbit. He slipped into the house and slammed the door.

17

Pooh picked Eeyore's tail up off the ground.

"If this thing means nothing to Rabbit," said Pooh,
"I think I'll find a use for it."

Meanwhile, Tigger was still trying to help Eeyore find
his tail. He was certain that someone had stolen it, but
who? Rabbit lived close by, so Tigger decided to question
him first.

Moments later, Rabbit threw open the door, and in bounced Tigger.

"Gotcha!" said Tigger, knocking Rabbit flat.

"What?"

"Where were you the night o' the forty-third?" demanded Private Ear Tigger. "When was the next-to-the-last time you saw Eeyore's tail?"

"Eeyore's tail?" repeated Rabbit. "What do you mean?"

As Tigger was explaining, Rabbit noticed that his Worm Wrangler was missing. It was another case for the Private Ear!

"But what about my tail?" asked Eeyore.

"Not now, Eeyore," said Rabbit and Tigger.

"Who was the last no-good-nik you saw?" asked Tigger.

"Why, it was Pooh Bear," said Rabbit. "But he's…"

"A case of Very Little Brain goin' bad!" declared Tigger.

Eeyore sighed. Wasn't anyone going to find his tail?

Winnie the Pooh was sitting on a branch by a beehive, about to fill his honey pot.

"My tummy tells me this is a Bee Tickler!" said Pooh, looking at Eeyore's tail. He stuck the tail into the hive and wiggled it around. Several bees fell out, laughing.

"I was right!" said Pooh, reaching inside. He crammed some honey into his mouth. The bees glared at him.

"Uh-oh!" said Pooh, gulping. "Tickle, tickle?"

The angry bees swooped down on Pooh and tumbled
him and his honey pot off the limb. Eeyore's tail landed on
a thorny bush.

"Oh, bother!" said Pooh as he fell. When he hit the
ground, the honey pot got jammed on his head.

"Is it time for a midnight smackerel already?" asked
Pooh. He couldn't see a thing. Then he tripped and
tumbled down the hill.

26

Pooh barreled into Tigger, Rabbit and Eeyore. When they rolled to a stop, Rabbit yanked Pooh's honey pot off his head.

"Tryin' to disguise yourself, Buddy Bear?" said Tigger.

"Where's my Worm Wrangler?" demanded Rabbit.

"What about my tail?" asked Eeyore.

"Not now, Eeyore!" said Rabbit and Tigger.

But Pooh knew nothing about a tail, or a Worm Wrangler. "I'm missing my Bee Tickler," said Pooh. "Perhaps Mr. Private Ear can help me find it."

"I love this job!" said Tigger, bouncing.

"Forward, men!" said Tigger. He peered under every rock and around every tree in the Hundred-Acre Wood. But he walked right past the bush where Eeyore's tail was hanging.

Piglet saw his friends hurry by and wondered where everyone was going.

"Oh, my!" thought Piglet. "Perhaps they're looking for s-something scary!"

Piglet suddenly spotted Eeyore's tail.

"Oh, d-dear! That certainly looks like a very small part of a Very Large Animal," said Piglet. Since Piglet was a Very Small Animal himself, he trembled fearfully and backed away. He backed into a branch behind him. Startled, he jumped up into the air and landed right by Eeyore's tail.

When Piglet saw that nothing was attached to the tail, he was relieved. He picked it up. "You might come in handy for protecting me from spookables!" he said.

When he reached home, Piglet made himself a Bully Bamboozler—a small Heffalump made from a balloon, with Eeyore's tail for a trunk.

Meanwhile, not far away, Tigger was thinking hard.

Who would want Eeyore's tail? "It has to be one pitiful little termite!" said Tigger.

"Piglet's little and pitiful," suggested Eeyore.

"Piglet! That's it!" said Tigger. He drew a "Wanted" poster that was supposed to look like Piglet, although it didn't. Then he bounced off to Piglet's house.

"Look!" said Pooh, pointing straight at Piglet's Bully Bamboozler. It looked like the fellow in Tigger's poster.

"Grab him!" yelled Tigger, pouncing on the balloon. There was a loud pop, and Eeyore's tail went flying.

Owl flew by at that very moment.

"My word!" said Owl, swooping down to grab Eeyore's tail. "This looks like my Uncle Torbett's bell rope!" And off Owl flew with his new prize.

Tigger looked up as Owl flew by with Eeyore's tail.

"It's time we get to the top of this mess!" said Tigger.

But all Eeyore cared about was his tail.

Tigger bounced up to Owl's house and pulled the bell rope right off the door. "They don't make them like they used to," said Tigger.

When Owl came to the door, Tigger bounced in and threw the bell rope down on a chair, accusing Owl of taking it. Eeyore backed into the chair and sat down sharply on the bell rope. When it stuck him, he jumped into the center of the room. His friends stared.

"My Worm Wrangler!"

"My Bee Tickler!"

"My B-Bully B-Bamboozler!"

"Uncle Torbett's Bell Rope!"

Tigger yanked off Eeyore's tail and held it up as evidence.

"I know no one cares except me," said Eeyore sadly, "but that's my tail!"

"Wait, Eeyore! That's it!" said Tigger. "Your tail plotted its own disappearance so you would learn to appreciate it! I knew it all along!"

Tigger pinned the tail back onto the smiling Eeyore.

"Well, from now on," said Eeyore, "my tail and I are going to stick together—no matter what!"